CONTROLLING HER PLEASURE

Under His Command Trilogy

Part One

By Lili Valente

CONTROLLING HER PLEASURE

Under His Control Trilogy: Part One

Lili Valente

Copyright © 2015 Lili Valente
All rights reserved.
ISBN-13: 978-1507821589

All Rights Reserved

Copyright **Controlling Her Pleasure** © 2015 Lili Valente www.lilivalente.com

All rights reserved. Without limiting the rights under copyright reserved above, no part of this publication may be reproduced, stored in or introduced into a retrieval system, or transmitted, in any form, or by any means (electronic, mechanical, photocopying, recording, or otherwise) without the prior written permission of the copyright owner.

This erotic romance is a work of fiction. Names, characters, places, brands, media, and incidents are either the product of the author's imagination or are used fictitiously. The author acknowledges the trademarked status and trademark owners of various products referenced in this work of fiction, which have been used without permission.

The publication/use of these trademarks is not authorized, associated with, or sponsored by the trademark owners. This book is licensed for your personal use only. This book may not be re-sold or given away to other people.

If you would like to share this book with another person, please purchase an additional copy for each person you share it with, especially if you enjoy hot, sexy, emotional novels featuring Dominant alpha males.

If you are reading this book and did not purchase it, or it was not purchased for your use only, then you should return it and purchase your own copy. Thank you for respecting the author's work. This book was previously published as Skin Deep by Anna J. Evans in 2009. It has been extensively revised and reworked before being re-released in serial romance format.. Cover design © by Violet Duke. Edited by Robin Leone Editorial.

Table of Contents

About the Book
Author's Note
Dedication
Also by Lili Valente
Chapter One
Chapter Two
Chapter Three
Chapter Four
Chapter Five
Chapter Six
Chapter Seven
Acknowledgements
About the Author
Sneak peek of Under His Command
Book Two, Commanding Her Trust

About the Book

* * **Warning:** This book features a big, tattooed, Dominant alpha male—give him your trust and he'll command your pleasure. All. Night. Long.* *

Blake Roberts has everything he's ever wanted—fame, money, and ownership of the hottest chain of tattoo parlors in the country. But he's haunted by his first love, the matching tattoo they share a constant reminder of who he was before he learned how to control his emotions, his desire, and a woman's pleasure.

He needs to purge her from his heart, and he'll do whatever it takes to be free.

Erin Perry's been burned by love and she's

not ready to put her body under a man's control, let alone her heart. But then Blake shows up, the only man she ever truly loved. Blake is ruthlessly handsome, and seething commanding energy that has her aching to submit.

To be pleasured, tamed, owned, and put under His control.

Author's Note

Blake and Erin's story is a fictional representation of a Dominant and submissive, BDSM relationship, based on research conducted by the author. In a real Dominant and submissive relationship, all sexual activity should be safe, sane, and consensual.

Dedicated to my D.O.M. who knows what that stands for. Thank you for helping proof this novel, even though you were worried it might give you a heart attack.

ALSO BY LILI VALENTE

CONTROLLING HER PLEASURE

COMMANDING HER TRUST

CLAIMING HER HEART

Learn more at www.lilivalente.com

PROLOGUE

Erin

She was nearly naked again, wearing nothing but tiny black panties, and his hands were everywhere but where she needed them to be.

Calloused fingertips traced the column of her spine down to the small of her back, deliberately avoiding the aching place between her legs as he gripped her thighs and pulled them apart.

Wide.

Wider.

Strong hands circled her ankles with a careless ownership that made a soft moan escape her lips.

"See there, Erin. Aren't you glad I caught you in time?" His voice was as rough as the rope he used to secure first one ankle and then the other to the bedpost behind her.

As he worked, Erin could feel her mind softening, sinking into a pool of cool, clear water even as her body caught fire.

Descending into submissive space, into that place in her mind where nothing mattered but one man and what he would command her to do, had always reminded Erin of floating. Drifting into a delicious dream where pleasure and pain fused together, where mind and body finally made peace with one another. Where her consciousness focused to a knifepoint and she finally felt completely alive.

Subbing was a better high than any drug

and three times as addictive. It was like flying without any fear of the fall.

At least not any fear until it was all over and it was too late to take back the parts of herself she'd given away.

"Tell me, Erin." He'd finished with her ankles and was now hovering above her prone form, braced on the hands he'd placed at either side of her shoulders.

He was close enough that she could feel his heat but not the comforting weight of his body and it was pure hell not to squirm beneath him, silently begging for what she craved.

His breath was warm against the back of her neck, his lips brushing lightly against the sensitive skin as he spoke. "Tell me what you want."

Erin shivered, but not because of the cold.

She'd grown accustomed to the chill in the cabin. Too bad she couldn't grow accustomed to what this man did to her or control her body's instinctive response to the Dominant he'd become.

Of course, even if he hadn't grown into just the kind of man her twisted libido craved like an addict craves a fix, just the fact that he was Blake would have been enough.

The familiar smell of his skin made her wetter than she'd been in years, the feel of his large hands moving to her wrists had her nipples drawn into tight, aching points, and the way he said "want" was nearly enough to make her come.

Right then, without as much as a fingertip between her legs.

And he knew exactly what he was doing to her.

The bastard.

"Fuck you," she whispered, the defiant words kicking her arousal into overdrive.

Unfortunately for her, the only thing more arousing than being obedient was being defiant. So she didn't fight him as he checked the cuffs securing her to the headboard.

Fighting only fueled the fire.

"No more fucking," he said, the surety in his voice underscored by the buzzing of the tattoo machine beside the bed. "No more distractions. We're going to finish this, sweetness. Right now."

Erin's pulse pounded unhealthily in her ears and a cold sweat broke out between her shoulder blades as she realized a needle could be only a few inches away from her skin.

It was sick, but even as her nerve endings sizzled with fear, her panties grew wetter.

"Tell me what you want, Erin," he said, his deep voice vibrating through the cool air. "This is your last chance."

But she didn't say a word. She only pressed her face into the cool quilt and waited for the familiar sting.

Waited for Blake to mark her flesh the way he'd already marked her heart.

LILI VALENTE

CHAPTER ONE

Twenty-four hours earlier
Blake

Did it still count as a kidnapping if she went with him willingly?

What if she wanted out of the car once she realized they weren't stopping inside the Los Angeles city limits? If he refused to stop, would that decision automatically make him a felon?

Blake didn't know. But he knew that, even at sixteen, Erin hadn't been easily intimidated. He couldn't imagine her sitting quietly beside him as he headed off into the middle of Bumfuck mountain country.

No matter how physically intimidating most of the population found Giant Blake Roberts of *Vegas Ink*, Erin would remember good old Blake from when they were kids. Back when he'd been a six-foot-two-inch beanpole with elbows bigger than his biceps who'd had his ass handed to him by their foster father on a weekly basis.

Erin would call his bluff. She would try to run, and if he didn't want her leaping out of a moving vehicle to gain her freedom, he'd have to use the rope he'd packed in his trunk.

Because she would do something like that. She'd always been wild, and from what he'd observed in the bar earlier tonight, she'd only gotten crazier with age.

Not that he was in a position to throw

stones.

What he was planning was more than crazy. It was stupid, criminal, and could ruin the life he'd worked so hard to build. If he knew what was good for him, he'd start up his car and get the hell out of here right now. Do not pass go, do not kidnap the only girl he'd ever loved, do not collect multiple felony charges.

"This is crazy. You realize that, right?" His best friend and business partner, Rafe, echoed Blake's thoughts before taking a long pull on his flask.

There was whiskey in there tonight, but Blake had decided to stick with a Coke while they staked out the staff parking lot of the bar from his car. No need to risk a DUI as well as abduction charges.

"You haven't seen her in how long?" Rafe asked. "Six years?"

"Eight."

Rafe exhaled, long and slow. "And she didn't respond to any of your letters?"

His teeth ground together. "Nope." Not

with words anyway.

Instead, she had ripped every letter into tiny pieces and mailed them back to his address in Vegas. She *had* responded, just not in a way that made him think she would be accommodating to what he wanted from her. What he *needed* from her whether she was willing to give it or not.

Blake wasn't usually the type to take what he needed without permission, but for Erin, the girl who had broken his heart into a thousand razor-sharp pieces, he would make an exception.

Rafe grunted and took another swig from his flask. "But you still think it's a good idea to show up where she works and ask her to go away for a long weekend so you can work on her tat?"

Blake nodded. "Yep."

His friend laughed as he clapped him on the shoulder. "You've lost it, man."

If he only knew...

But Blake hadn't told Rafe his real plans.

No need to make his best friend an accessory to a felony and ruin two lives instead of one.

"Who knows? She might enjoy a little vacation," Blake said, not believing the words even as he spoke them. "Or maybe I'll be able to change her mind about the money. Fifteen grand isn't chump change and she must need cash. Why else would she be working here?"

"Maybe she's slumming." Rafe shrugged as his dark eyes scanned the parking lot of the bar where they'd finally found Erin.

It wasn't in a bad part of the greater Los Angeles area, but it was the raunchiest place still serving drinks in Pasadena. Most of the town had been converted into one big outdoor mall, purely PG stuff, but The Elbow Room had managed to stay open.

Probably because it was the one place in the sleepy suburb where a man could still see some skin while he slammed back a few beers.

The oversize bar doubled as a stage for drunk college girls, looking to add their bras to the collection hanging from the ceiling, and the bartenders were scantily clad ex-porn stars from the Valley. They took turns dancing on the bar on nights when the coeds were hitting the books instead of the bars. Except Erin. She wasn't part of the porn scene. She was a lingerie model for the biggest fetish store in Los Angeles.

Or had been at one time.

Blake hadn't seen any new pictures of the stunning natural blonde with the big hazel eyes for nearly two years. Not that he was a glutton for punishment, who checked the Damned Naughty Lingerie website on a weekly basis…

God, what was he doing here?

Obsessing over Erin's picture on a website or writing her letters was one thing. But tracking her down in person with the intention of forcing her to take a trip up to the San Bernardino Mountains with him was certifiably insane.

Exactly. So get out of here. Now. Before this woman ruins your life a second time.

"I don't know, man. She's not slum material," Rafe said, his tone revealing his obvious appreciation for Erin "Angel" Perry. "It's hard to believe this girl can't get modeling work anymore. I checked out the site this morning. I've never seen real tits like that. No wonder you're still hung up on—"

Blake silenced Rafe with a look.

No one talked about Erin that way, even his best friend.

It didn't matter that she'd betrayed him and broken his heart back when he was a stupid kid. He wouldn't tolerate anyone treating her like a piece of meat, even if he were planning to do nearly the same thing himself.

But then, he'd earned the right to teach Erin a thing or two about payback.

"Listen, Blake." Rafe sobered, his features settling into a serious expression. "I know you're a big boy and can take care of yourself, but this has bad idea written all over it."

"Exactly, so get lost already," Blake said. "Before you get too drunk to drive yourself back to the hotel."

It was twenty minutes until The Elbow Room closed for the night. He had to get rid of Rafe before then.

Rafe sighed. "Well, if you ask me, you shouldn't be wasting your time or your money on shit from the past. The future's golden, brother."

"I didn't ask you. For your opinion or your company." In fact, he'd done his best to ditch his friend, but the other man had insisted on accompanying him to L.A.

"Easy, killer." Rafe lifted his arms at his sides. "All I'm saying is that we could be in Miami getting pussy right now instead of wasting time in smog city."

His Cuban accent colored the city's name so it sounded like some exotic mecca. Which it was, in a way. At least for the two of them.

After three years as stars on the reality show *Vegas Ink*, they had quit the entertainment biz to go national with a string of tattoo parlors. The Vegas Ink locations in

Reno and Vegas would stay open and be joined by new locations in Memphis, New Orleans, and Miami.

Blake and Rafe were going to cash in on their celebrity status and cement their reputations as the best of the best, *the* people to trust when you were looking for more than your average ink, when you wanted certifiable body *art*.

"You've got a matching tattoo with the chick, Blake, and she managed to cash in on it. That doesn't mean she's got a piece of you." Rafe barreled on, despite the warning look Blake shot in his direction. "You were young. You made a mistake and got burned. Who cares if—"

"I care." Blake took another swig of his own drink, the warm, sickeningly sweet Coke as foul as his mood.

If he hadn't already been determined to go through with his plan, what he'd observed tonight would have done the job. He'd only stepped into the bar for a few minutes, but it had been enough to see everything he needed to see.

Erin still had the tattoo he'd given her the night before his eighteenth birthday, peeking out from beneath her sleeveless white shirt. Not that it came as any surprise.

She'd used the tat to make a name for herself and clearly hadn't been impressed by Blake's letters asking her to have the piece modified. After all, his work had been as responsible for her nickname as her angelic good looks.

The five-inch figure on her shoulder was the first of the angel tattoos Blake had later become famous for, an exact match to the wide-eyed fallen angel on his own forearm. It was the only one of his tattoos he hadn't sketched himself and the last remaining example of his father's work.

Adrian Roberts had never made a living or a name for himself before his death, but he'd been a real talent, a more gifted artist than Blake could ever dream of being. More than anything in the world, Blake wished he could go back to that night when he was ten years old and grab more than one of his father's sketches before he ran from their burning apartment.

Maybe then he'd have more of his dad, the only real family he'd ever had, to hold on to and wouldn't be so damned obsessed with this one tattoo.

Or with the girl he'd once loved enough to share a piece of his soul with her.

Your soul? It's just skin. You should know that better than anyone.

Ah, but there was the kicker. He *should* know a lot of things. But right now, all he knew was that he had to convince Erin to let him cover the tattoo, to rework it into something no longer recognizable as the same angel on his own arm.

It made him sick to know she still sported the profession of his adolescent love on her shoulder.

Once the evidence of his foolish belief in

soul mates was erased, Blake was certain he'd finally be able to let go of his obsession with his former flame and move on.

Cultures across the world recognized the mystical power of working permanent ink into human flesh. Blake had never been one to believe art was anything more than art, but he couldn't deny the connection he felt with the only person in the world with whom he shared the exact same ink.

A connection that had haunted him for eight long years as he tried to forget about the last night they'd shared and the promises they'd made. Promises Erin had broken as easily as she'd broken his heart.

Your broken soul, your broken heart. God.

You're right. You need to do whatever it takes to get this girl out of your system so you can stop being such a fucking pussy.

"Are you laughing?" Rafe asked, obviously as surprised by the phenomenon as Blake himself.

"Yeah." He smiled and downed the last of

his soda. "I was thinking about Delilah and her pussy lecture."

"The one about the power of the pussy to give life and pleasure and how we shouldn't use the sacred name of her vajayjay as an insult?" Rafe asked, his contempt for their Vegas office manager's feminist rants clear in his voice, though his expression softened perceptibly.

No matter how often his partner insisted his decision to transfer Delilah to the new Miami location along with them was purely good business, Blake suspected Rafe had a thing for Dee and would cut off a finger or two to get into her holy vajayjay.

Too bad Delilah couldn't see through Rafe's macho bullshit to the solid man inside. She actually seemed to have a thing for Blake and had asked him for drinks on more than one occasion, but he'd always declined.

Blake didn't mix business with pleasure. And even if he did, he didn't feel anything but friendship for the magenta-haired manager.

He'd never felt anything but friendship, or lust, for any woman but one, and it was past time he did whatever it took to get *her* out of his system.

He was twenty-six years old, for God's sake. It was time to get the hell over his high school love and that wasn't going to happen while they shared the same ink.

He'd tried everything he could think of to stop thinking about Erin and their matching tattoos—hell, he'd even gone to see a therapist a few times—but nothing helped.

Something had to be done.

Now.

He was on the fast track to having everything he'd ever wanted and he wasn't going to waste another eight years of his life fixated on the one who got away.

"Speaking of the power of the pussy, I think it's time for me to head back to the hotel," Rafe said. "See if I can snag a starlet or two at the bar."

The two men got out of the car, slamming

the doors behind them.

Rafe glanced up at him in the dim light of the parking lot's street lamp. "You sure you won't come back with me?"

Blake shook his head. "Nope. See you in a few days."

"Or a few minutes, if she turns you down." Rafe paused at the door to his BMW roadster. "You know what, I think I'll come in. See what she—"

"No. I'm doing this alone," Blake insisted. "I don't want to be recognized."

Rafe laughed. "Are you kidding me? You're Giant Blake Roberts. People are going to recognize you. With or without me."

"You think people at a bar like this watch Brava?" Blake asked, happier than ever that their reality show hadn't been on one of the major networks.

A certain degree of celebrity he could contend with, but being recognized everywhere he went would have driven him insane.

"Besides, I'm undercover." He pulled his hat lower on his face and tugged down the arms of his black sweater, concealing his full-sleeve tattoos.

Without them, he was a fairly average-looking guy with short dark brown hair, dark brown eyes, and unremarkable features. Not ugly by any means, but his wasn't the face that had kept female viewers glued to the screen for three seasons of *Vegas Ink*.

Rafe was the pretty boy. If anyone were going to be recognized, it would be him.

Blake doubted even Erin would be able to guess his own identity, at least not right away. He'd shot up three more inches and gained about eighty pounds of pure muscle since the last time she'd seen him.

Unless, of course, she watched the show.

Blake hadn't allowed himself to think much about that, to imagine she might be sufficiently interested to follow his life. Thinking like that was a great way to let this situation get out of hand.

He wasn't here to reconnect with her; he was here to right a wrong and move on with his life. End of story.

"I'll have my cell if you need me," Blake said, a grim smile on his face as he shoved his wallet in his pocket.

"I'll be in Miami by tomorrow afternoon. I won't need anything." Rafe slid into his roadster and slammed the door.

But it was only a second before he rolled down the window. "Call me if you come to your senses and want to be on the flight tomorrow morning, man. Okay?"

Blake nodded, but it was too late to come to his senses.

He was committed to this plan and to a life without memories of Erin haunting him and the sooner he got what he came for and put this behind him, the better.

CHAPTER TWO

Blake

Blake waited until Rafe's car was out of sight before walking around to the front entrance to The Elbow Room.

There was no longer a doorman on duty at this hour and the crowd inside had thinned considerably since ten o'clock.

As Blake strode across the worn plank floors, the bartender, with her long black hair pulled back in a braid, announced last call. But the clutch of men surrounding the bar looked far from ready to call it a night.

Why would they, when Erin was holding court on top of the bar and growing increasingly daring with her dancing?

Her shirt was hiked up high enough to reveal the bottom of her bra and her thumbs tugged her skirt lower as her hips swiveled, revealing her hip bones and the pale skin below. State regulations expressly forbid the bartenders from stripping, but Blake expected clothes to start coming off any second.

An expectation obviously shared by the men surrounding her like a pack of dogs.

His hands tightened into fists, his body itching to defend Erin the way he had when they were kids.

Back then, she'd been an innocent fourteen-year-old kid attracting the wrong kind of attention from the senior boys at school.

They'd known she was a foster kid and had no one to look out for her. She'd been cornered behind the gym within three days of transferring to Carson City High. By the time Blake came around the corner of the building, her three attackers had stripped her down to her bra and panties and were pinning her to the gum-pocked concrete.

Blake had earned himself two weeks of detention for beating the shit out of the football players who had decided it would be fun to pass around the new girl, but it had been worth it.

No one had messed with his foster sister again.

He wouldn't even allow himself to touch her until she turned sixteen, though she'd made her interest clear long before then.

"Kiss me, Blake," she whispered, tilting her head back to look up at him as they watched the sun sink behind the horizon outside of Carson City. "I want

you to be my first kiss."

"Not tonight," he said, even though he was already so hard his jeans felt like they were cutting him in half.

But they'd been passing a forty of Budweiser back and forth for the better part of an hour and Erin's eyes were glassy. He didn't want their first kiss to be like this—something she might not even fully remember.

Besides, she was only fifteen and so innocent, no matter how tough she tried to play it.

Until she'd been placed with Phil, she'd had it relatively easy for a foster kid. She still remembered what it felt like to be loved, to be important to someone who cared about her with no strings attached.

But those memories were fading fast.

He could see it in the way her shoulders curved as she slunk past the lockers of the boys who had nearly raped her. He saw it in the tears she refused to let fall after Phil slapped her for talking back one time too many.

She needed Blake to be her no strings attached person more than she needed a boyfriend. He knew that.

He also knew that once he kissed Erin it would be hard as hell to keep from doing more. He hadn't been innocent for a long time and he wasn't sure how long he'd be able to control himself with this girl who'd won his heart without even trying.

He wanted to touch every inch of her soft skin. He wanted to know what sounds she made when she came. He wanted to get his mouth between her legs and show her all the things he'd learned how to do during months of making out behind the bleachers with the biology substitute last year.

"Then when?" she asked, leaning into him, not realizing the sweet torture she was inflicting as her breast brushed his arm. "I want to kiss you so much. I just…love you, Blake. You're the best person I ever met."

His heart turned over in his chest.

He loved her, too, and he was grateful she'd come into his life and reminded him how good it can feel to love someone before it was too late.

But he couldn't let friendship go any further, not yet.

Not until he proved to himself that he was as good a man as Erin thought he was.

And so he'd held her at a distance for months that felt like eons of erotic torture.

Blake had been nearly two years older and hadn't wanted to take advantage, no matter how many nights he had lain awake with a raging hard-on, fantasizing about the girl sleeping in the next room.

Apparently Erin still had the power to inspire a similar reaction in him and any other member of the penis-possessing segment of the population.

Blake was going to have to watch his step. Pulling Erin away from her pack of horny and delusional admirers was likely to make tempers flare and he couldn't afford to attract that kind of attention. He needed to get Erin out of here without anyone taking notice.

That meant he'd have to stay in the shadows and watch, bide his time until she was finished with her performance, no matter how torturous a part of him found it to see Erin bumping and grinding for a bunch of horny drunks.

Or how arousing the other part of him found it.

Damn, but she was even sexier than he remembered.

The way she tossed her long hair over her shoulder, flashing those big eyes in a way that promised untold pleasure to every man in the room—it made his entire body ache. It was going to be hellish to be trapped in a cabin with her for three days without being able to touch her, kiss her, be buried deep inside the only woman who had ever—

Who ruined your life. Focus, Roberts.

His inner voice was right.

He had to focus because there was no turning back now.

Soon he would be leaving Pasadena with Erin by his side, either as his passenger or his captive.

At least *that* choice would be hers to make.

LILI VALENTE

CHAPTER THREE

Erin

Five more bucks from her regular Carl, three from a thirty-something Latino guy, and two from his girlfriend.

Combined with the twenty she'd lifted from the frat boy too drunk to see what he was fishing from his wallet, the money she'd made in the past ten minutes brought Erin up to an even four hundred for the night. It made it worth the anxiety she felt every time she took her turn on top of the bar.

And it was more than enough to pay for an entire hour of very expensive attorney time…if she ever got the guts to hire the woman she'd met with last week.

Erin knew Scott expected her to sign the divorce decree as it stood. He would bust a blood vessel if he learned she was considering hiring representation to fight him in court. Her soon-to-be ex-husband was *that* certain of his ability to scare her absolutely shitless.

Of course, he had every reason to be sure of himself. She had rarely dared to stand up to him during their three-year relationship. Back in the beginning, she'd thought he was the man of her dreams. But back then, she'd been a naive single girl in the big city and there hadn't been so very much at stake.

But she couldn't think about any of that now. She had to concentrate on raking it in, doing whatever it took to part the men surrounding her from the last of their cash before her shift ended. And if that included getting a little creative, so be it. She didn't particularly enjoy having a stranger suck a body shot out of her belly button, but what she enjoyed didn't matter.

Nothing mattered anymore except reclaiming her life from the man who held it hostage.

"Time for a shot!" Erin forced a naughty smile onto her face as she pulled her shirt even higher, baring more of the bottom of her bra.

The little white schoolgirl top tied at the waist, combined with the shortest kilt she could find, was always a recipe for big tips. Cliché as it might be, men still went crazy for a schoolgirl uniform, especially if you were willing to lie down and let one of them suck alcohol off your stomach while wearing it.

"Pick me, Angel!" someone drunkenly called from the opposite end of the bar as she poured the cinnamon liqueur into the well of her navel.

"Not tonight, gentlemen," she said, winking at the Latino guy's girlfriend. "I'm in the mood for a softer touch."

A new song came over the sound system and Erin clapped along as the blushing girl with jet black hair and warm brown eyes sidled up to the bar. The roar of the men cheering as the petite woman held back her dark curls and suckled the Goldschlager from Erin's stomach was too loud for her to tell for certain, but the song sounded like vintage Rolling Stones. One of her favorite bands of all time.

Hell, she might actually be enjoying herself right now if she were just getting a little wild on a Friday night, instead of playing the tart for a crowd.

It had been so long since she'd been able to just go dancing, to hit a club or a bar for fun with some girlfriends. Not that dancing at The Elbow Room was torture. She'd never been shy about her body, and her time as a celebrity lingerie model for Damned Naughty Lingerie had made her even less so.

Still, she wished she didn't have to be on display every night. At least not right now, when she still felt so vulnerable.

Screw it.

Suck it up and give the customers what they want.

As soon as the girl's lips left her stomach, Erin hopped back to her feet and finished out the song with her usual flair. She swiveled her hips and bent over far enough to give the patrons a glimpse of her white cotton panties with the lace trim, fueling enough naughty into her moves to keep the men panting, but keeping it clean enough that the crowd didn't get out of hand. It was an art—walking that fine line—but one she'd perfected in the past month.

She worked her way up and down the length of the bar one last time, collecting another twenty bucks before the closing bell sounded. Moments later, "Happy Trails to

You," the bar's signature closing song, began to play and Erin stopped dancing, drawing sounds of protest from several of the drunker patrons.

"See you tomorrow, gentlemen," she said with a grin and a flutter of her fingers.

Always leave them wanting more.

"Hey, Angel, can you clean up the well?" Cassandra shouted from where she was loading the last batch of glasses into the dishwasher behind the bar. "I've got everything else ready to close."

"Sure thing," Erin said, already feeling the familiar exhaustion that washed over her at the end of the night, once the adrenaline rush was over.

She pulled her shirt down and was preparing to hop down from her perch when a large hand closed gently around her ankle. Her first instinct when customers tried to take looking at the goods to the next level was usually a slap on the wrist and then a kick somewhere more painful if they didn't wise up fast. But for some reason, the feel of this hand was different, intriguing.

Electric…

Then she heard the voice that went with the hand and dry panties were a thing of the past. "Nice tattoo. What I can see of it."

Damn. A voice like that, so deep it practically had its own reverb, was almost enough to make her forget she'd sworn off men for the next ten years. Or twenty, depending on the day and how much time she'd had to think about Scott.

"Thanks. It made me famous," she said, smiling down into the shadowed face of one of the biggest men she'd ever seen in real life.

He was six and a half feet tall, at least, and the way his arms and chest stretched out his sweater left no doubt he was strong enough to snap her in half without breaking a sweat. The very thought of something like that should have been enough to cool her rapidly heating blood, but it wasn't. She was a hopeless case when it came to big, strong, domineering men.

Even after three years with a Dominant man who had made her life a living hell and taken away everything that meant something to her, a part of Erin still fantasized about finding someone man enough to take control of her the way a real Dominant would. The way she'd seen some of the men at the clubs treat their subs. With respect and even love.

Like their submissives were precious things to be treasured, protected, and valued, not lower life forms as interchangeable as sheets of Kleenex.

"I think you've got a few other things going for you other than a tattoo," the man said, his thumb caressing the inside of her ankle, sending a sizzle of awareness racing up her leg.

God, she'd never been so glad she chose heels instead of her fuck-me boots.

Though those could have been good, too. She could already see herself pulling this man into her tiny studio in South Pasadena and taking off everything but her boots. Then she'd turn around, lean over the bed, and show him how wet she was, how ready to take whatever he was packing in those black jeans. He wouldn't say a word, or maybe he'd just tell her to spread her legs a little wider. Then he'd be behind her, large hands gripping her hips, thick cock spearing inside where she was—

"You want to go somewhere?" the man asked. "Talk?"

"We've got to close up," Erin said, the tremor in her voice betraying where her thoughts had been headed. "But I know a diner not too far from here. We could get a coffee."

"I'd love a coffee. My car is in the back lot," her mystery man said, reaching a hand up to help her off the bar. "I could give you a ride."

Oh, dear, she just *bet* he could give her a ride.

She hadn't even seen his face, but he

practically radiated sex. Controlling, demanding, *completely-dominating-the-woman-he-was-fucking* sex. The kind she'd been craving for nearly two years during her Scott-imposed celibacy. Two years without even the comfort of another warm, human body, let alone the fucking she craved.

A good *fucking*—not lovemaking, not even gentle sex—that's what she wanted.

What she needed. Erin was a carnal person, always had been. She needed it rough, hot, and primal, and it was past time for her to scratch that itch.

Tomorrow she would be back here, working another double shift. But tonight was for her. Or even better yet, for him. There was nothing she enjoyed as much as bringing a big man like this to his knees with pure, unbridled lust.

Erin smiled, wishing she had the guts to skip coffee and head straight back to her apartment with a total stranger, but even two years of celibacy hadn't made her that daring.

Of course, she could at least clue this guy in on what she was hoping they would get around to doing after coffee…

Ignoring the hand he held out, she leapt straight into the big guy's arms, looping her hands around his neck and her long legs around his thick waist, bringing her panties into intimate contact with his even thicker cock.

Damn. This guy was as big below the belt as he was everywhere else. And he was hard, hot, and ready, so erect she could feel him throbbing against her even through his jeans and her damp panties.

"Looks like we're on the same page," she said, breath coming faster as she flexed the muscles in her legs, urging her clit into even tighter contact with his cock. "And I really hope you are up for…" Her words trailed away and the heat coursing through her was replaced by a wave of ice cold fear.

Oh, God. Why hadn't she made sure she got a good look at this man's face before she jumped him like a nympho on roofies?

"Something wrong, Erin?" Blake Roberts asked as he set her down on the ground.

Several seconds passed in awkward silence before she could remember how to form words. And once she did, only two words came to mind.

Holy.

Shit.

CHAPTER FOUR

Erin

Of *course,* the first man she'd decided to sleep with since her breakup would be the one man she never thought she'd see again.

It was Blake. And, whoa, if he hadn't grown up in all the right places.

Back in high school he'd been sweet,

loveable, and sexy, but now he was…

"Why don't we get out of here? We can go for a drive, catch up. Go get your things," he said, his tone revealing there would be no argument.

Trouble. That's what he was. Big trouble.

And damn if that didn't make her panties even wetter.

"I don't think that's such a good idea, Blake," she said, moving slowly behind the bar, concentrating on capping the well liquor, no matter how much a part of her wanted to hasten to obey him.

But then, she supposed some sub tendencies died hard.

"We haven't—" She broke off with a nervous flutter of one hand. "I mean it's been years and— I-I've just got a lot going on right now, and I—"

"It's just a ride," he said in that deep, sexy voice of his. "And a talk."

"That's not what it felt like a few seconds ago." She blushed, cursing the shot of Jack

Daniel's she'd tossed back before her last turn on the bar.

This was all the whiskey's fault. She never would have jumped into a stranger's arms and started rubbing herself all over him without it.

She might have *wanted* to, but she wouldn't have actually *done* it.

"That was a few seconds ago." He smiled, and she caught a flash of the skinny boy who'd appointed himself her protector from the second they met, making her wonder how much he had really changed. "I came here to talk old times not relive them. Though I wouldn't put up a fight if you decided you wanted more than talk. Seems we've still got the same chemistry."

"Seems like it," she said, finding it easier to return his grin.

She capped the last of the well drinks and eased out from behind the bar, highly conscious of Cassandra's eyes on her and Blake.

The other bartender had been giving her

shit for weeks, begging Erin to let her set her up with an eligible screw or two. Now Erin could practically feel the "go for it" vibes surging toward her from across the room.

Unfortunately, Blake wasn't any more her idea of eligible than the ex-porn star crowd Cassandra hung with.

"But that's probably not a good idea," she said. "Sometimes it's nice not to have any history."

He made a considering noise low in his throat. "Sometimes you're in the mood for a stranger."

"Yes." She nodded, grateful he understood.

He didn't seem angry or disappointed, either. In fact, he was amazingly casual about the whole thing. If she hadn't felt how hard he'd been, she would never have guessed he was interested at all. Which was a good thing, she supposed, though she couldn't deny a certain disappointment.

"But other things are better with an old friend." He stepped closer, forcing Erin to tilt her head back to keep looking him in the eye.

When he spoke again, his voice was soft, almost a whisper. "Come on, let's go for a ride."

"Go, Angel," Cassandra said in a knowing tone as she wiped down the bar. "I'll finish closing up and Pedro's still in the break room. He'll walk me to my car."

Erin hesitated for the barest moment more.

There was a voice inside her that urged her to forget she'd ever seen Blake, grab her purse, and call a cab to take her back to South Pasadena alone. But it was a quiet voice, one that couldn't compete with her curiosity.

Why was Blake here?

Why had he tracked her down now, after all these years?

She had to know. Besides, Blake was the most trustworthy person she'd ever known. Hell, one of the only trustworthy people she'd ever known. If he said he was cool with talk and nothing more, he meant it.

And she was strangely exhilarated by the

thought of just taking a drive with this man.

But then, some of her best memories were of being in the car with Blake, racing down the desert back roads, imagining they were on their way somewhere, anywhere but back to Carson City, Nevada.

"Let's just keep going," she said, hanging her head out the window and letting the hot desert air whip it into a wild tangle.

"Where should we go?" Blake asked, playing along, the way he always did. "Rome? Paris?"

She laughed as she reached out, threading her fingers through his much longer ones. "I don't need Europe. Give me Denver. Or maybe Miami. Someplace hot where we could live in swimsuits and have sex in the ocean every day."

Blake's grip tightened on her hand and his jaw clenched. "You're killing me. You know that."

She leaned in, pressing a kiss to his cheek before she whispered. "No, you're killing you. I'm so ready, Blake. I want more than your fingers or your mouth. I want you. Inside me. Tonight." She reached her free hand over, caressing him through his jeans, her breath rushing out as she felt how hard he was. "God, baby, I want you. Please, tonight. Please... Make love to me under the sky and then let's get back in this car and keep driving until the sun comes up."

"Okay," he whispered, finally giving her what she'd been begging for. At least the first part.

He made love to her until she felt like she'd died and been reborn in his arms, until she was even more in love with Blake Roberts than she'd been before. And even when he'd turned the car around and headed back to their foster home, she hadn't been too sad about it.

Phil was a nightmare, but she had the dream of being in Blake's bed every afternoon before their foster father got home to look forward to.

The memory of those long afternoons spent learning how to drive Blake as crazy as he drove her made Erin's decision for her.

"Okay, let's go for a drive," she said. "Just let me grab my purse."

LILI VALENTE

CHAPTER FIVE

Blake

"So, what brings you to L.A.?" Erin's bare feet were propped on his dashboard, just like in high school.

Her long legs were the same shade of tan, but this time the tiny moon-shaped toenails were painted a deep black instead of cherry red.

Black like her soul, man. Don't forget it.

But it would be so easy to forget. To forget what he'd come for, what they'd been to each other, and to forget the dreams she'd abandoned when she'd hauled ass out of Carson City the morning after his eighteenth birthday.

From the second she'd jumped into his arms in the bar, he'd wanted to forget it all. To forget and to *fuck*. To strip away those white panties she was wearing and get balls deep in Erin.

She'd been more than ready for it, before she'd realized who he was. Even then, she'd still agreed to go for a ride. She might very well be up for heading to the nearest hotel. They could check in for the weekend and he could have her in every filthy way he'd imagined for the past eight years. Maybe that alone would be enough to get her out of his system.

And then, come Monday morning, he could drop her back in the parking lot of the bar and be done with his obsession forever.

"Is it business?" she asked, reclining her chair until she was lying almost horizontal in the passenger seat beside him. "Or pleasure?"

Blake's eyes flicked to the newly bared skin at her midriff and then quickly back to the road.

Jesus, who was he kidding?

One weekend would never be enough. The second he felt that hot, tight little pussy encasing him, he'd be a goner.

Fucking Erin Perry had been an unparalleled pleasure and he was sure fucking Angel Perry could become a bona fide addiction. She'd had eight years to perfect what had been an amazing natural aptitude for sexing a man's soul from his body, and just the way she'd danced on the bar made it clear she'd been hard at work mastering her seduction skills.

"I'm guessing business if I know you." Erin let one of her knees relax outward, giving him a clear view of her panties.

God. Damn. They were modest as far as women's lingerie went and looked like sensible cotton, with just a hint of lace at the edge. They weren't anything fancy or seductive. But just knowing Erin's hot little cunt was beneath those granny panties was enough to get him hard enough to shatter glass.

"Something to do with that show you're in?" she asked. "I've never seen it, but I've heard you're great." Her legs squeezed back together, depriving him of that glimpse of white fabric, which was probably a good thing.

He should be keeping his eyes on the road. California drivers took no prisoners. You were expected to be going eighty miles an hour and tailing the driver in front of you close enough to count the dents on their bumper, or it was grounds for a drive-by. Even at past midnight, Interstate 10 was hopping, packed with cars headed to Palm Springs and destinations beyond.

He needed his attention on the traffic, not his passenger.

Thankfully the streetlights beside the highway would disappear in a few miles, once they were out of the city. Then it would be too dark to obsess about what Erin was or wasn't revealing.

"So do you like being a reality television star?" she asked.

Blake shrugged and moved the car into the carpool lane. In California, two people counted as a carpool. No wonder the traffic was so brutal.

"I thought you said we were going to talk while you drove?" she asked, a hint of amusement in her tone. "Don't tell me you've turned into a real man and can't do two things at the same time."

He smiled in spite of himself. Erin had always been able to make him smile when no one else could. "You haven't asked where we're going."

"Maybe I don't care where we're going,"

she said, following the words with a sigh sadder than anything he'd ever heard out of her mouth.

It was just the tiniest exhalation of breath, but it spoke volumes. Even back in the day, when she'd been the new girl at Casa de la Hell—Blake's nickname for his final foster home—she'd never been anything but upbeat and sassy.

Erin defined sass. She'd more than done her part to earn the occasional backhand from their foster father, Phil.

Phil. Such a fucking friendly name for such a demented bastard.

Blake wouldn't have blamed Erin for running away from that man. If only she'd told him where she was going…

"I've got a cabin up in the mountains, not too far from Lake Arrowhead," Blake said. "We'll have privacy there. We can hang out, drink a few beers, watch the snow fall."

Now was as good a time as any to fill Erin in on his plans. Even she wasn't crazy enough to jump out of the car while he was doing eighty on the interstate. It's when they turned off the highway that he'd have to get out the rope—assuming she wasn't any more accommodating to his in-person request than she'd been to his letters.

"I got the letters you sent back to me, by the way," he said, ready to get that out in the open, as well. "That was a mature response."

"I'm sure it was." She laughed, but it was a short, bitter sound, not at all like the old Erin. "Unfortunately, it wasn't mine. I haven't been receiving my mail for a long time. Well, the past few weeks I've been getting mail at my new apartment, but nothing from you."

Blake was quiet, taking in the information, knowing she would clarify if he stayed silent. Erin always divulged information in bits and pieces. Stories burst from her like hiccups, interspersed with other random information unrelated to the matter at hand.

"You hungry?" she asked. "I'm dying for a burger. With onions. Lots of onions, the grilled kind."

His lips twisted in a bittersweet smile. At least some things were still the same.

She reached down, fiddling with the controls on her seat until she was nearly upright again. "My soon-to-be ex-husband intercepted all of my mail. He was very…controlling."

"That why he's going to be your ex?" Blake asked.

"That's part of it," she said, her tone making it clear she would rather not talk about the man.

Fine with him. Blake didn't like to think of any man in connection with Erin. Part of his own set of mental glitches.

"So what did the letters say?" She sounded uncertain and strangely…hopeful.

Blake risked a look at her side of the car, but now it was too dark to see her expression clearly. "Just hello from an old friend."

She snorted. "Bullshit."

"How do you know? You didn't read

them." But he couldn't keep from grinning. This could actually work out. If Erin hadn't been the one to rip up his letters, she might be open to having the angel tat modified.

"My bullshit meter still works fairly well. Most of the time." She laughed, a lighter sound this time. "So what else did the letters say, old friend?"

Shit.

He actually wished they weren't driving now that he knew Erin hadn't heard his request. This was the kind of thing more comfortably discussed if you were sitting down, looking someone in the eye, not driving down the highway.

But here is where they were.

"I was asking if you would be open to having me modify your angel tat." He kept the words casual, but he could feel her surprise in the beat of silence that followed.

"Why?"

Here was the tricky part, the part so much more easily communicated in a letter. Good thing he wasn't the type of man who could only do things the easy way.

"Obviously things didn't work out the way we planned when we decided to get identical tattoos, Erin," he said, trying not to think too much about the kids they'd been or how much he'd once loved her. "That's fine by me. You made your choice and I respect that. But I've come to a place in my life where I'd rather not have a matching tattoo with a woman I don't even know anymore."

"And you can't change yours because of your dad," she said, making a considering sound beneath her breath. "That's a sucky position to be in."

"Only if the woman in question isn't open to having me modify the tattoo." Casual, just keep it casual. "I've got all my stuff in the car, ink and—"

"This is hardly a car. It's an Expedition, for God's sake." She laughed as she stretched out her legs and still didn't touch the back of the floorboard. "It's like half of an eighteen-wheeler. Lot different than that Impala you had in high school, huh? Bet it doesn't die every three days."

"I'm one of the best in the business now," Blake said, refusing to be distracted. "I was an amateur when I did that work on your shoulder. Now, I've got the skills to give you something really beautiful and unique."

"Though I did like that car," Erin said, crossing her legs on the seat as she reached down to the floor for her purse. "It had personality."

"And don't worry, I'll do it for free."

She sucked in a breath and let it out through pursed lips. Even before she spoke, Blake knew he wasn't going to like what she had to say. "No, you won't," she said, her tone serious. "You won't do it at all. I'm sorry, Blake, but I'm not going to change the tattoo."

His jaw clenched. "Would fifteen grand change your mind?"

She did a double take. "Are you trying to

bribe me?" She seemed angry for a second, but when she spoke again, her voice was soft, almost defeated sounding. "You know what? It doesn't matter, because, no, it wouldn't."

"I understand it's become a big part of your professional persona, but—"

"It *is* my professional persona," she said, returning to rifling through her purse.

"Like I said in the bar, I think you have a few things—"

"My name is Angel now, for God's sake. Not legally, but it might as well be." She flipped down the visor and opened the mirror, causing light to spill across her face, showing him how sincerely troubled she seemed. "That's what I'm known as and the tat is a big part of what I'm known *for*. I'm just now trying to get back into the modeling business after two years. I can't change one of the most memorable things about me."

"That's understandable," Blake said, not losing hope just yet. "What if I reworked it so that you still had an angel? I could lengthen the wings, change up the colors, maybe even add some darker hair on one side so it looks like she's facing—"

"I can't," Erin said as she smoothed on a coat of berry-colored lipstick. No, gloss, that's what they called the stuff that made a woman's lips shine like she'd just been kissed, or just had her mouth smeared with—

Nope, not going to let his mind go there. Erin was going to be pissed when she realized he didn't plan to take no for an answer. There was no chance she'd still want to go to bed with him, and he wasn't the type to take what wasn't freely offered.

Except control over what she's going to have tattooed on her skin for the rest of her life. Isn't that just as bad?

"You can, Erin, and you will. I'm going to modify your ink this weekend." He forced the words out through his tight jaw, refusing to listen to the voice of reason. "If you decide what you want by Sunday afternoon, I'll do my best to accommodate your request. If not…I'll decide for you."

"You're fucking kidding me." But the way she flung her lipstick back into her purse with enough force to make it bounce back out again made it clear she knew he wasn't kidding.

He lifted one shoulder. "This is something I feel strongly about."

"Yeah? Well, I feel strongly about getting the hell away from—"

His hand whipped out, closing tight around her upper arm, not hard enough to bruise, but firm enough to let her know he meant business. "Don't touch that door handle. You'll kill yourself if you jump out of a car going eighty. Do you understand me?"

"Yes." She shivered lightly in his grasp and Blake felt the tension suddenly leave her body. She slumped slightly in her seat, her lips parting and her eyes sliding closed.

Goddamn, but she looked almost…aroused.

Like she'd gotten off on the controlling

way he touched her. Like she enjoyed…

But he had to be misreading things. Erin was one of the toughest girls he'd ever known, pure steel beneath the sass. She was a fighter, a scrapper, not a submissive, and there had been nothing in their early relationship to hint she wanted to be dominated.

But then, she'd said her ex-husband was "controlling," and he couldn't ignore the way her body language had changed when he'd pulled out the Big Bad Dom voice, the one the girls around the Vegas parlor jokingly called his "Yes, Daddy" voice. It was the one he used in the Vegas bondage clubs when he needed to indulge that side of himself, the part of him that needed to command another's pleasure to fully experience his own.

Could Erin…

Just maybe…

There was one way to find out.

LILI VALENTE

CHAPTER SIX

Blake

"Put your purse on the floor," Blake continued in the same firm voice.

After only a beat of hesitation, Erin obeyed, making his cock twitch with excitement inside his pants.

Down, boy.

She might just be scared. It might have nothing to

do with sex.

It was true. She might just be intimidated.

Sometimes he forgot his mere size alone was enough to frighten people, even without the scary voice. He'd never been the kind of person to use his bulk as a tool to get what he wanted. Still, it was something he had to consider.

He loosened his grip on her arm and softened his tone. "I have some questions. Will you answer me honestly?"

"Yes," she whispered, her voice thick with what sounded more like desire than fear.

"Are you turned on right now?" he asked.

She shivered again and her breath caught, but she didn't speak.

"Answer me, Erin," he said, his cock swelling inside his jeans. "Are you turned on? Tell me the truth."

One beat, two, and then the word he didn't realize he'd been afraid to hear until she said it. "Yes."

Oh. Fuck.

This wasn't good. He'd been right about what Erin wanted, but it would be so wrong to act on what he'd learned. Any Dominant and sub interaction should be based on respect and trust.

He would never enter into even a casual scene with a sub with any agenda other than shared mutual pleasure. To use this to control Erin, to persuade her to let him alter her tat, would be wrong.

But then…he didn't have to abuse the knowledge. Once they arrived at the cabin, he could go back to treating her like an old friend and keep all persuasive efforts aboveboard.

Or at least above the waist.

Right now, however, he had thirty more miles before he'd be out of urban areas and onto the dark mountain road leading to his cabin. He couldn't afford to have Erin jump to her freedom or risk the chance that someone might notice a girl tied up with rope in his backseat as he drove through downtown San Bernardino.

And he could think of the perfect way to occupy her busy little hands, to keep those fingers so focused she wouldn't even think about going for the door handle.

"Are you wet?" he asked before he had the opportunity to talk himself out of his decision.

"Yes." Erin moaned softly and Blake saw her hands clench into fists on her lap.

Oh, yeah. She was more than ready for what he had in mind. It was clear in every tense line of her body.

"In a few seconds I'm going to tell you to touch yourself," he said. "When I do, I want you to slide your fingers in and out of your pussy. Play with yourself until you're hot and wet. Will you do that for me?"

"Yes." She spread her legs wider and Blake had to fight the urge to turn off at the next exit and find the nearest motel.

His cock was already ridiculously hard, his balls aching like he'd been sucker punched between the legs. He was going to walk like he'd been riding bareback by the time they made it to the cabin.

But then, that was only fair.

He deserved to suffer, especially considering what he had in mind for Erin.

"I want you to touch yourself everywhere and anywhere it feels good." He paused for a moment, his own desire spiraling higher when Erin stayed perfectly still, waiting for his command.

She was obviously no newbie and understood the kind of pleasure that came with bending her will to another's.

"But don't touch your clit," he continued. "That part of you is mine for the next hour. If you come without touching it, that's fine. But if you disobey me, if you run even a pinkie finger over it, I'll know. And you'll be punished. Do you understand?"

"I didn't agree to punishments and we don't have a safe word," she said, her voice breathy with excitement.

"No, you didn't, and no, we don't. If that

bothers you, we can stop right now." He sounded surprisingly calm considering how desperately a part of him wanted Erin to obey him, to let him guide her to her pleasure.

He could already picture her with her head thrown back, her eyes closed as she drew closer and closer to coming on her own hand, could practically hear the sound of her eager fingers delving in and out of her slick cunt.

"Is that what you want?" he asked.

A brief pause and then she sighed, relaxing back into her seat. "No…sir."

The addition of the typical sub term of respect sent another jolt of need surging down to his already aching cock.

"Good," he said. "Now put your hand down the front of your panties. I want to be able to smell how wet you are by the time we hit the San Bernardino exit."

Erin spread her knees and lifted her skirt, giving him a clear view as she slowly slid her hand beneath the white fabric and over her mound. She moaned as she pressed her fingers deep inside her channel, the sound so thick with need he had no doubt it had been a while since Erin had indulged this side of herself.

Was that because of her ex?

Had he been one of those sadistic types who got off on making his sub's life a living hell? Blake had met his share of Doms like that, cowards who needed to walk all over another person to make themselves feel like men.

They were the kind of assholes who gave genuine Dominants a bad name. Blake had never entered into a full-time commitment with a submissive, but if he ever did, his girl would be treated with nothing but kindness.

True, sometimes "kindness" could take on unconventional forms in the BDSM world, where even punishments and pain could be considered kind if they were what the sub needed to get off, to feel safe and cared for. Blake had played with a number of women who needed to be spanked, told they were dirty whores, or bound and gagged and fucked with what most people would say was a lack of gentleness in order to experience their greatest pleasure.

But he'd never hurt a woman.

He'd never left his lovers with emotional or physical scars.

Not like the kind Erin had acquired, if the tears streaming silently down her face were any indication. Even as she played with her pussy, clearly aroused by what she was doing, she wept.

He could practically feel the pain inside of her fighting her pleasure, and it was enough to make his heart wrench uncomfortably in his chest. She'd been through something, something bad, and she was still suffering from the side effects.

Could he add to that pain? Even if she had betrayed his trust? Was he *that* mentally screwed up by the almost mystical connection he felt to the only person with whom he shared identical ink?

Unfortunately, the answer to all three questions was yes.

"You're safe, Erin. Nothing's going to happen that you don't want to happen. At least not until Sunday afternoon," he said, ignoring the flash of conscience the last words inspired.

"Relax," he continued in a soothing voice. "Concentrate on your pleasure, on getting my pussy as wet as you can make it."

Damn, he'd staked a claim without meaning to.

But then, it was hard not to think of her pussy as *his*, especially when he knew exactly how he was going to reward her obedience, with his face between her legs, eating that pussy until she came so hard she couldn't remember her own name.

It had always felt like Erin was his, a part of him ingrained so deeply he worried that not even eliminating their matching tattoos would force her out. Or that, even more disturbingly, he even *wanted* her out.

Get it together, Blake.

This weekend is about taking back your life, not getting even more obsessed with a woman who couldn't care less about you.

It was true.

A part of him wanted to believe Erin had loved him back when they were kids, but if she had cared that much she wouldn't have acted the way she did. She wouldn't have promised him forever and then run as fast and as far as she was able the very next day.

He had to follow through with what he had planned, no matter how tempting it would be to play power-exchange games with Erin all weekend and forget why they were shacked up in a cabin in the middle of nowhere.

He'd picked the location because he didn't want anyone to see or hear if she wasn't cooperative, but it would also be the perfect place to stage a private scene.

No one would be able to hear her scream when she came, again and again, on his face, his hands, his cock, his—

"God, Blake. I'm so wet," she said, squirming restlessly on the seat beside him. "Are you going to fuck me?"

"Do you want me to fuck you?"

"Yes…please." She moaned again, and her hand moved faster between her legs, driving in and out of her slick heat, but not touching her clit. She was being obedient, doing her best to earn his approval.

"I want you to fuck me," she said. "Hard."

Shit.

Hard.

That was exactly what it was going to be to resist losing himself in Erin.

As hard as the erection pressing so fiercely against his fly that Blake swore he could feel the metal teeth of his zipper through his boxer briefs.

CHAPTER SEVEN

Erin

Erin felt like she was going to die.

Right here, right now.

Spontaneously combust from the force of her sexual frustration. On her headstone they would write, "If only she could have gotten off before it was too late."

"Please…please, Blake."

Erin moaned, moving her hand faster, driving fingers into the aching, bruised place her pussy had become. She'd never been so hot or so wet, never been poised on the verge of a shattering orgasm for so long without being able to come.

It was torture.

Pure, horrible, *wonderful* torture.

"Just a few more minutes. There's a place to turn off the road and park in about half a mile." Blake's voice was maddeningly calm as he steered through the almost complete blackness of the mountain road.

She wanted to slap him.

And then fuck him.

She wanted to rip open his pants and straddle him, riding his cock while she sank her teeth into the thick muscles of his shoulders. She wanted to feel his strong hands digging into the flesh of her hips, highlighting her pleasure with a little pain.

And then she wanted him to punish her for biting him without permission, have him turn her over his knee and redden her ass until—

"God. Please! Now!" She couldn't take much more, and her lurid thoughts certainly weren't helping any. Her breath was coming in swift, shallow pants, and her entire body felt like one screaming exposed nerve.

She needed to come.

Now. Not in a few more minutes.

"Lower your voice, sweetness." And then he slowed down, until it felt like they were crawling up the side of the mountain in a freaking horse-drawn wagon.

There was no one else on the road at nearly two in the morning. He could drive ten miles an hour if he wanted, make sure they didn't reach that turnoff until morning if she weren't obedient.

God.

Damn. Him.

Erin pressed her lips together, the part of her that wanted to tell him to go fuck himself warring with the part of her that was willing to do *anything* it took to win Blake's approval.

From the second he'd used that deep, silky Dom voice on her, she'd been a goner. No matter how freaked out she'd been that the sweet boy she'd once known had turned into the kind of man who would tattoo another person against her will, that shock had faded to the back of her awareness once she'd realized what else he'd become.

Dominant.

Wonderfully, perfectly Dominant.

In the past forty minutes, he'd controlled her more completely, more skillfully than Scott had managed in three long years. It was more than the tone of his voice, or the way he kept his cool no matter how she'd tried to tempt him into putting an end to her torture with a quickie in the back of the Expedition—and she had tried every dirty trick she could think of that didn't expressly violate Blake's order not to touch her clit.

It was something else, something she couldn't quite put her finger on, that made her want to please Blake, to be a good sub in a way she never had been before. He emitted an aura of Dominance, one that reached out and surrounded her in bliss when she was pleasing him and froze her blood in her veins when she was not.

The odd sensation made her feel connected to him.

It was like they'd already made love, even though he hadn't so much as breathed on her skin.

Making love…

Whoa. No way.

She was *not* going to go there.

She would submit to Blake, she would fuck Blake, but there would be no *lovemaking*. She didn't need the complication of that particular emotion. Even if she did, Blake would never want to make love to her, the way they used to all those years ago.

She'd broken his heart and her promises, two things she'd known even the eighteen-year-old Blake would never forgive, let alone the hardened man he'd become.

The realization was enough to cool her lust a few degrees until he spoke again.

"Take off your shirt," he said. "I want to see you play with your nipples."

Oh. God.

He knew how sensitive her breasts were, how she'd been ready to head for a home run the first time she'd let him get to second base in the back of his Impala. Just a few minutes of playing with her nipples and she'd been wet and ready, practically dying to feel Blake inside her, no matter how lousy her first few experiences with boys had been.

"Now, Erin. Make them hard for me." He reached out with one hand and gently undid the top button on her shirt. "I want your nipples tight when I take them in my mouth."

She couldn't get the damn shirt off fast enough.

Her bra followed a second later, and then her hands were on her already aching tips, squeezing, caressing, rolling her nipples between her fingers and thumbs until they stung. The slippery wet heat from the fingers she'd had in her pussy smeared across the pebbled flesh, adding to her pleasure until she was squirming in her chair.

"Blake. Please, Blake," she whispered, squeezing her thighs together, seeking relief from the erotic torture he was forcing her to inflict upon herself.

His eyes flicked from her breasts to the road and his breath finally began to speed.

He wanted her.

So, God, why wouldn't he take her? If she had to wait a second longer to feel his cock in her, she was going to scream.

Or take matters into her own hands.

Every sub had a breaking point and she was reaching hers.

"Don't do it, Erin," he warned as if he'd read her thoughts. "We're almost there. Keep your hands on your tits."

"I hate the word 'tits,' " she snapped, her tone a cross between a whine and a growl.

How had he known?

She hadn't made any sign she was planning to move her hands.

He chuckled, a deep rumble she felt vibrating her already humming nerves. "Really? You're not a tit girl?"

"Fuck you. You know I am. I just don't like the word." For a split second, she wondered if Blake would revoke her ability to speak for her rebellious tone, but the bastard only laughed again.

"That's a shame. I like the word 'tits.' "

She could imagine the shit-eating grin he had on his face though she couldn't see more than his profile in the dim moonlight.

"I'd especially like it if I were fucking your mouth," he continued, "pumping between those pretty lips. I'd like to tell you I was about to pull out and come on your tits."

Oh. My.

Erin's entire body shuddered.

"Then I would, hot and thick all over your soft skin," he said, ratcheting up her desire another impossible notch. "I'd rub my cock all over your chest, spread my cum on your nipples, play with you until I was hard again and then push your pretty breasts together and fuck your tits.

Would you like that, Erin? To have me fuck your tits while you played with yourself?"

She almost came right then.

The man was a dirty-talking master. Before she could remember the words she needed to tell him just how hot the idea of him fucking her tits made her, he spoke again.

"Take off your panties, but leave your shoes on," Blake said as they rounded a curve in the road and a lookout point came into view. "We're here."

Erin had never been so thrilled to see a parking area in her life.

Or so scared.

What was wrong with her? This is what she'd been dying for since the second Blake told her to put her hand down the front of her panties.

Why was she suddenly scared of what was

going to go down between them? She wanted this, needed him more than she'd ever needed almost anything.

There's your problem. And that's after less than two hours with the man.

What state are you going to be in after two days?

But there was no time to listen to the cautious part of her mind. Blake had already pulled into a space near the guardrail at the edge of the observation area.

"Get out of the car," he said. "Put your hands on the hood and spread your legs," he said as he pocketed the keys.

Erin shivered. "But I'm not wearing a shirt."

"Get out of the car," he repeated calmly. "Put your hands on the hood."

"And it's freezing outside," she said, even as she reached for the door handle.

She was stalling.

She didn't really care about the cold or the threat of being caught half naked. Hell, she found the idea she might be seen incredibly arousing. But it was as if the knowledge that they were *really* going to have sex had finally penetrated her lust-fogged mind.

She was going to have sex. For the first time in *two years*.

With *Blake*.

Her Blake, one of the only people she'd ever let inside her heart, and one of the many people she'd let down in her relatively short life.

What if he secretly hated her for it?

What if he'd never forgiven her for leaving Carson City without telling him?

Was she risking getting even more mentally screwed up than she was already by allowing him to dominate her, to trust him with her well-being while she was in such a vulnerable place? What if he—

"Don't worry," he said, reaching out, running his knuckles softly down the curve of her jaw.

She still couldn't see his eyes, but the gentle tone of his voice spoke to every last one of her doubts. It was as if he'd known, once again, what was going through her mind almost before she did.

"I'll keep you warm." He brushed the pad of his thumb across her lips. "Now get out of the car. I'm ready to fuck my pussy."

Erin stumbled out of the car, the cold wind taking her breath away for a second.

There was a big difference between mountain temperatures and Los Angeles temperatures in the winter months. They were less than three hours from the city, but there was already at least a thirty-degree drop in temp and it was bound to get colder as they drove higher.

She didn't even have a pair of jeans to cover her legs, let alone a coat or the kind of shoes she would need if she were to try to run from Blake. Of course, that was probably part of the reason he'd chosen the San Bernardino Mountains.

They were sparsely populated in the winter months and her inappropriate clothing would keep her bound to him, ensuring that she remained his captive.

That realization should have scared her, but instead it only intensified the aching between her legs. The idea of being held against her will, at least by Blake, was painfully arousing.

Which just went to show her libido was even more twisted than she'd assumed.

"Hands on the hood, sweetness, let me feel how wet my pussy is." Blake's large, warm body was behind her then, blocking the wind, enveloping her in his energy, banishing thoughts of anything but him.

Erin placed her hands on the engine-warmed hood. No sooner had her fingertips made contact with the Expedition than Blake's fingers were between her legs, making her cry out with relief. Just his touch was enough to banish some of her desperation, to take her that much closer to completion.

He groaned softly as he played through her folds, feeling how her slickness ran down the insides of her thighs, how her lips were plumped and swollen with the force of her need. Down one side of her pussy, and up the other, he traced every inch of her aching flesh until finally his finger brushed lightly across her clit, making her knees buckle.

"Blake," she cried out, knowing she would have fallen if he hadn't looped a strong arm around her waist, catching her, holding her upright as he continued to tease her nub with a gentle, insistent pressure.

"God, you're so wet," he murmured, his lips teasing against her neck, making her ache even more powerfully. His hand moved away from her pussy, an action she was about to protest before she felt him working at the close of his pants behind her. "Do you still want my cock inside you?"

"Yes, please, yes." Tears of relief rolled down her cheeks and her entire body began to shake with anticipation.

Finally!

It felt like she'd been waiting years for him, for his touch, for the feel of his cock falling, hot and heavy, out of his pants, pressing between the cheeks of her ass.

"I'm going to fuck my pussy now, Erin." Blake's breath was warm against her cheek as he whispered through her hair.

Erin heard the sound of foil tearing and then, seconds later, felt the blunt head of Blake's cock at her opening. "Tilt your hips."

She obeyed and then, a moment later, he shoved inside her. His thick cock stretched her inner walls to the limit, filling her completely, owning every inch of her pussy with just one swift thrust.

Erin moaned with the pleasure, dizzy from the familiar feel of him, the smell of him, the rightness of being bared to Blake. The cold air, his warm body, and the molten heat of his cock were nearly enough to take her over the edge. Then he moved his fingers over her clit, and she was falling.

She screamed as she came, her knees bending, feet coming off the ground as her orgasm ripped through her body with a force unlike anything she'd ever known.

Her channel pulsed and clutched at where Blake lay, still buried deep within her. Her nails clawed into the metal beneath her hands, and her nipples practically burned with raw sensation.

Every inch of her skin was on fire, consumed by the bliss of the release so long denied her.

Things low in her belly contracted, tighter and tighter, until it was almost painful. Her clit pulsed and throbbed beneath Blake's firm touch, making her gasp for breath. In seconds her head was spinning, lights dancing behind her closed eyes as she rode the waves of the orgasm that had taken control of her, body and soul.

No, not the orgasm. *Blake.*

Blake was the one in control. In perfect, restrained, dominant control, a fact he made clear as he pinched her clit between his fingers and whispered in her ear, "Come again, Erin. Right now. Come on my cock."

And she did.

Oh, God, she did, another blinding release even more powerful than the first.

Tears were running down her face by the time she came back into her skin, feeling her soul had become too big for her body and yet too small at the same time. She didn't fit inside her flesh the way she had before and it was frightening for a moment, but then Blake took care of that, too.

"Put your feet on the ground." As soon as she obeyed, wobbling slightly, still unsteady on her feet in her heels, he started to fuck her.

Not make love, not have sex.

Fuck.

He rammed into her cunt without mercy, slamming forward with such force that she had to brace herself on the hood and push back against him to keep from being glued to the side of the car. It wasn't romantic; it wasn't emotional.

It was hard, fast, brutal. In a word—perfect, exactly what she needed to ground herself back on earth. And to come near the edge of completion for a third time.

Erin spread her legs a little wider and shoved back against Blake as he thrust forward, intensifying the penetration until she could feel the head of his cock making bruising contact with the end of her pussy.

The hint of pain made another rush of wet heat flow between her thighs and Blake groan behind her. His hands flipped up her skirt and took hold of her hips, digging his fingers into the full flesh of her ass.

"Harder, harder!" Erin begged, gasping for breath as the tension within her built to a level she'd never dreamed possible.

She was either going to come again or shatter into a million pieces, and she didn't really care which.

As long as Blake kept fucking her.

Touching her.

Taking her.

"Don't come. Not yet. Wait for me. Wait," Blake demanded, even as he obliged her by squeezing her ass even tighter.

"Oh, God. Oh, God." Erin struggled to obey, but oh, fuck, it was hard.

She was so close, so terribly close, and he felt so amazing. His cock actually seemed to be getting thicker as he neared his own release, stretching her pussy even farther, making her feel so full of him that there was room for nothing else.

Nothing but Blake.

And it was perfect, better than anything she could remember, even the other times she had been with him.

"Now. I want my pussy to come now." He punctuated his words by jerking her hips back toward him.

He forced himself so deep inside her that the hint of pain as he met the end of her was enough to make her wince—wince and come like the world was ending in a big burst of fire.

"Fuck! Blake!"

She screamed the words and a few other

things she couldn't remember as her mind spun inside her skull like she'd slammed back half a bottle of Jack Daniel's and her pussy did its best to squeeze Blake's cock in half.

She moaned as he jerked inside her, each tiny movement enough to take her even higher. She'd never felt so connected to a lover, as if his pleasure were her own, as if every wave of his release triggered a ripple of bliss inside her.

It was more than she'd ever expected, more than she knew what to do with as she finally drifted down from the high of her first triple orgasm.

Triple orgasm.

She'd come *three* times and Blake hadn't even seemed like he was trying that hard. What would he be capable of if they became regular lovers again, if they had the time to re-learn the little things that—

What the fuck are you thinking?

He doesn't want to become lovers; he despises you so much he can't stand the idea that you share a matching tattoo and is willing to permanently alter the damn thing without your consent.

Get your head on straight and figure a way out of here before it's too late.

"Get back in the car and warm up. We're still about twenty minutes from the cabin," Blake said as he pulled out of her, the loss of contact between them as depressing as her inner monologue. "Thank you…for your trust."

He kissed her softly on the top of her head as he smoothed down her skirt, but the affectionate gesture did nothing to stop the anger slowly flowing into her veins, replacing the euphoria of a few moments before.

Thank you for your trust.

Her trust?

That was it? No "You were amazing" or "That was the hottest fuck of my life"? Or even a "Damn, I can't wait to have you again"?

No, he just wanted to thank her for *her trust.*

Wasn't he the big, bad, unavailable Dom?

Just like Scott had been during the first year of their marriage, when he still made love to her but never had a kind or affectionate word. Never made her feel like anything but a sub in the worst sense of the word.

Subhuman.

That's what she'd been to Scott, and what she'd vowed she'd never be to any man, ever again.

The headlights came around the curve only a second later. It was as if some higher power had heard her thoughts and decided she deserved a chance at deliverance.

Erin ran for the road without a moment's hesitation, heedless of her nudity or of Blake's voice behind her, ordering her back to the car.

Fuck him and his orders.

She was getting the hell out of here.

In less than a few hours, he'd gotten under her skin to the point that his lack of pillow talk after they'd had sex had hurt her.

What kind of damage would he be able to

inflict in a few days?

Erin had no idea, but she wasn't sticking around to find out.

Her heels clicked madly on the pavement as she dashed for the road, racing the heavy footfalls behind her for salvation.

Get ready for more heat, more suspense, and more big, bad Blake Roberts in COMMANDING HER TRUST, Under His Control Book Two.

Keep reading for a sneak peek.

Acknowledgements

I really do have so many people to thank, so please forgive my gushing in advance.

Big thanks to my husband, my biggest fan and most tireless supporter. You believed I could do this when not many people did. Love you hard man, forever and ever. Let's never go our separate ways.

Thank you to my critique partners (the most patient women in the world) for reading numerous drafts and never getting tired of Erin and Blake (or at least not letting me know they were tired of them).

Thank you to my editor, proofers, and sweet and lovely cover designer—this wouldn't have been possible without you!

Big huge thanks to all the readers out there. You are rock stars. The way you go above and beyond to support the authors you enjoy is truly amazing and so appreciated. Much, much love and endless thanks for embracing a newbie and making me one of your own.

Mad thanks to Kara H. for keeping me organized and on task. Without your help, professionalism, and all around awesome the launch for the Under His Command series wouldn't have gone one fifth as smoothly. You are the best!

Thanks to all the early reviewers who took a chance on Controlling Her Pleasure. I appreciate your time and effort to post ratings and reviews so much.

Finally a few special shout outs:

To my street team: You are the sweetest, naughtiest, book-loving-est people ever and I feel so lucky to have you in my life.

To Lauren Blakely who is a genius and a talent and just as importantly, a woman with a kind and generous heart. Thanks for being a friend and inspiration.

To Monica Murphy. Who would have thought we'd be here when we met in 2005? Can't wait to hang out with you again soon and soak up more of that signature MM sweetness and sass.

To Sawyer Bennett, a talented and generous new friend who constantly inspires me to be a better, more chill person. You make it look easy, doll.

To Violet Duke for the amazing cover

design, friendship, and support—even though I write naughty books and yours are so sweet and wonderful they make me laugh and cry in equal measure. You are a blessing to all who know you and that's the truth.

To Robin, friend and editorial guru, you make me laugh and keep my commas under control. Without you I would wander in the darkness of WTF punctuation-ville.

To my mother, who told to me to write whatever I wanted to write and pay no attention to the naysayers. What a lucky chick I am to have a mama like you.

To my father, who didn't live to meet my husband, babies, or book babies, but who raised me to believe I could do whatever I set my mind to, as long as I was willing to work hard and never give up. Thank you, Dad. You are missed more than you know.

And on a much lighter note, thank you to all the makers of chocolate in all its wondrous forms. You lift me up on days when the sun doesn't shine.

Tell Lili your favorite part!

Lili loves feedback from her readers.

If you could take a moment to leave a review letting her know your favorite part of the story—nothing fancy required, even a sentence or two would be wonderful—she would be deeply grateful.

Reviews are so important and help other readers discover new authors and series to enjoy.

LILI VALENTE

About the Author

Lili Valente started writing naughty books in her early twenties as a way to unwind after a long day in the day job trenches. She soon learned there was nothing more fun than torturing fictional characters who have dynamite chemistry in the bedroom.

After a prolonged detour through other areas of writing and publishing—including a short stint as a news reporter for a small town paper—she's back to penning red hot stories and loving every minute of it.

She lives on an island in the middle of nowhere, where she eats entirely too much fish and drinks more than her fair share of dark, island rum.

Lili has slept under the stars in Greece, eaten dinner at midnight with French men who couldn't be trusted to keep their mouths on their food, and walked alone through Munich's red light district after dark and lived to tell the tale.

These days you can find her writing in a tent beside the sea, drinking coconut water and thinking delightfully dirty thoughts.

Lili loves to hear from her readers.!

You can reach her via email at lili.valente.romance@gmail.com

Or like her page on Facebook https://www.facebook.com/AuthorLiliVal

ente?ref=hl

You can also visit her website: www.lilivalente.com

Or sign up for her newsletter here: http://bit.ly/1zXpwL6

LILI VALENTE

Commanding Her Trust
Under His Command
Book 2

Warning: This book features a Dominant alpha man who will push your boundaries until you beg for more. Read at your own risk.

Blake Roberts is falling hard for his old flame and won't stop until Erin is his. He doesn't simply want her body; he wants her submission, her abandon, and the wounded heart she's trying so hard to hide.

He wants all of her and he's pulling out all the stops—in the bedroom and out—until she surrenders.

For Erin, what started as a charade has become all too real. She's never experienced anything like the savage bliss she's discovered in Blake's arms. He tests her, dominates her, and if she doesn't gain her freedom, soon he'll own her—body and soul.

She has to escape even if running from Blake feels like running from the only home she's ever known.

Please enjoy this free excerpt of
COMMANDING HER TRUST,
Under His Control Book Two

Available March 2015 via Createspace, Amazon, and Barnes and Noble.

LILI VALENTE

CHAPTER ONE

Blake

Blake watched the ancient pickup pull off onto the gravel at the road's edge and ran even faster, determined to catch Erin before she got inside.

Before she took her life in her hands trying to get away from him.

It could be anyone in that truck. Some mountain man who hadn't seen a naked woman in years, a couple of drunk teenagers who would take turns raping the woman they'd picked up on the side of the road before dropping her off on the streets of San Bernardino.

Or even worse, there could be a bona fide psychopath driving that vehicle: a man who would have his fun with Erin and then kill her, dumping her body in the surrounding wilderness where it might never be found.

Or maybe the driver is a nice grandmotherly type who will buy her some clothes before taking her to the police station to file a report against the man who kidnapped her.

Erin skidded to a stop as the driver's door whipped open.

"Help, please I…" Her voice trailed off as an obese man in tattered overalls leveraged himself out of the vehicle.

"You need help, darlin'?" he asked, weaving as he lurched toward the front of the trunk, pursuing Erin as she backed away. "I'd be happy to help."

Despite the chances of being convicted of a felony, a part of Blake wished it *had* been a sweet granny in the truck.

Now he was probably going to come to blows with a man, who looked like an extra from *Deliverance*, to keep Erin safe. *And* he had a witness who might report what he'd seen to the authorities.

Not that it mattered.

If Erin decided she wanted to press charges, he didn't intend to try to stop her. Despite what the voices in his head had been telling him lately, Blake wasn't a psychopath.

At least not yet.

If this drunk did anything to Erin, however, Blake was going to lose what was left of his sanity.

"No one needs help." Blake's teeth ground together hard enough to make something in his jaw pop as he watched one of the man's large, meaty hands reach toward Erin's chest. "Get back in your truck."

"I wasn't talking to you, asshole," the man

said, still leering at Erin. "Come here, sugar and let me keep you warm."

"Get back in your truck," Blake repeated as his fingers closed around Erin's elbow and pulled her behind him, shielding her nakedness with his body.

"Fuck off," Overalls said, beady eyes narrowing on Blake's face. "The lady asked for my help."

Blake cursed himself.

Why the hell had he demanded Erin take off her shirt? She was irresistible enough clothed.

Of course, he hadn't thought anyone would see. It was the middle of the night, for God's sake, and most people knew better than to try to navigate the treacherous mountain roads after dark, especially after hitting the bottle.

But he could smell the whiskey on this character from three feet away, which gave him an idea…

"All right, don't get back in your truck," he said with a shrug. "I can smell the alcohol on your breath from here. And I doubt this will be your first DUI. Put your hands on the hood."

Blake heard Erin suck in a breath behind him as she caught on to what he was doing.

"I'm taking this one in for attempted prostitution," he added, jabbing a thumb over his shoulder. "It won't be any trouble to haul you into the station at the same time. I'll get her cuffed in the backseat and come back with some cuffs for you, Mr...."

"Uh um...Beam. Walter Beam," the man said, backing toward the door to the battered pickup. "But I haven't been drinking, officer. I swear."

"Great. You can prove it when I get back with the Breathalyzer."

Blake turned around, urging Erin in front of him, whispering as he went, "Get in the backseat."

"Prostitution?" She hissed though she seemed relieved to have escaped "Mr. Beam's" attentions.

Mr. Beam. It didn't take much imagination to guess Beam was the brand of whiskey he'd been drinking, not the name on his license.

"Do I look like a prostitute?" she asked.

"I don't know. What does a prostitute look like?" Blake asked, not surprised to hear the pickup roar to life behind him and tires squeal as "Walter" took off down the mountain like a bat out of hell.

"I don't know, you're the one who lives in Vegas. I heard it's legal out there," she said, shivering as he opened the Expedition's door and urged her inside. "That was a sad cop act, by the way. I thought you had your own television show. I expected better than 'haul you into the station.'"

"It was a reality show. I just had to be myself, not act like anyone else." Blake reached into the front for Erin's bra and shirt and tossed them into her lap. "Put those on and don't run away from me again. You could have been seriously hurt."

"You've got to be kidding me." The car's

overhead light illuminated Erin's face, revealing the flush that heated her cheeks. "*I* could have been hurt?"

"What do you think Walter would have done to you?"

"I don't know," she said, with a frustrated huff. "Taken me back to town?"

Blake tipped his head. "Maybe, but not before he took advantage."

"Took advantage?" She laughed as she finished up with her bra, but her hands were shaking as she reached for her shirt. "He might have copped a feel. At most."

"He might have raped you," Blake said, anger making his voice even deeper.

"He might have tried," she said, returning his glare, making it clear she wasn't scared of his angry voice. "But I can take care of myself, Blake. In case you don't remember."

"Then why didn't you get in the truck with him?" he challenged. "If you were so sure he was a safe bet?"

"I guess I didn't want to see what you'd do

to the poor guy if I did," she said, her eyes glittering in the dim light.

"I mean, you're the person who's kidnapping a woman so he can make permanent alterations to her body," she continued. "And you used to love *me*. Who knows what you might have done to some man you don't even know?"

The bravado in her tone made him sure she was simply reaching for the words that would hurt him the most, but they still cut deep. The way she'd known they would.

She wasn't stupid, his Erin. Volatile, emotional, and often too impulsive for her own good, but never stupid.

"I did love you. Enough to believe everything you said to me the night before you ran away," Blake said, careful to keep the emotion out of his voice. "And I don't hate you now. I hope you know that. I don't want to hurt you."

"Tattooing someone against their will is bound to hurt," she said, her voice still hard, though he'd seen the flash of guilt on her face when he'd mentioned the night she'd fled Carson City. "Literally hurt, and probably do a pretty decent job of destroying any *trust* you've built with the woman you fucked against the hood of your car."

"Trust," he echoed, letting the word linger between them. "Is that what this is about? You regret letting me dominate you?"

Erin's eyes dropped to her fingers and she suddenly seemed very interested in the workings of the buttons on her shirt.

"Answer me," he insisted. "Do you regret what we did?"

She sucked in a deep breath and let it out on a sigh.

"No," she mumbled, still not looking him in the eye.

"Then why did you run after we finished?" he asked, certain he was on to something.

This wasn't about her trying to get away from him because she was afraid or didn't want her tat modified. It was about the power games they'd begun to play, the amount of trust she'd given him so readily.

The trust that had floored him, aroused him, and come closer to softening the walls he'd built around his heart than anything had. Anything or anyone, even Erin herself eight years ago. If he were a smart man, he'd turn the car around and take her back to Los Angeles right now. No amount of ink modification was going to give him peace if he let Erin get under his skin again.

Too bad he was an idiot where this woman was concerned.

"Finished," she said, hurt obvious in her tone. "That's a nice way to put it."

"I'm sorry. What do you want me to say?" Blake asked, ignoring the tightness that gripped his throat. "After we had sex?"

"Fucked would be fine. That's all it was, right?" She looked up, her face carefully blank. "A little fucking between friends?"

She was hurting, that was obvious—he wasn't fooled by her controlled expression.

But how much of that pain had to do with what he'd done and how much was the result of her obviously troubled past, he couldn't say. But he could apologize, and try to make things as right between them as he could before they were holed up alone together for forty-eight hours.

"It was more than that. You know it, and so do I," he said. "I'm sorry if what we shared left you feeling confused, but you can't tell me you didn't enjoy it. Or that you didn't need it."

"What do you know about what I need?"

Blake sighed, recognizing her defiance for what it was, a mask for the fear many submissives felt when starting a relationship with someone new. He certainly hadn't meant to "start" anything or inspire those kinds of feelings in Erin, but now he had no choice but to deal with them.

"Listen, it's natural to be anxious about giving yourself over to another person, even if that person is someone you used to know very well," he said, keeping his tone soft and reassuring. He wanted her to know she was safe, that he wouldn't abuse her trust, and all his cards were on the table. "Especially if you've been in a relationship where you've been taken advantage of."

Erin tilted her head back, lifting her face to his, staring deep into his eyes without a trace of fear or deference.

At that moment, she was the least submissive woman he'd ever seen. If he hadn't experienced dominating her himself and seen how she reveled in being controlled, he never would have believed she was the type who enjoyed the lifestyle.

"You don't know anything about my former relationship, and you don't know anything about me," she said, every word clipped and deliberate. "Not anymore. So don't pretend you do. Just because we had sex, it doesn't give you the right to psychoanalyze me. I'm not some pathetic sub who needs someone else to tell me how I'm feeling."

Blake stared into her big brown and gold eyes, seeing so much more than Erin realized. "Is that what he taught you? That to submit is weak and contemptible?"

Without meaning to, he found himself cupping her cheek in his hand, then sliding his fingers into her impossibly soft hair.

God, how many times had he dreamed of feeling that hair falling around his face as he kissed this woman again? And here she was, so close, but still so incredibly far away.

She was everything he craved, but as forbidden as she'd been years ago when they'd both been too young to realize even true love could vanish in the blink of an eye.

Printed in Great Britain
by Amazon